The Pea Patch Jig
Thacher Hurd

Crown Publishers, Inc.

NEW YORK

A Head of Lettuce

Where the pole beans climb, where the tomatoes grow fat, where the onions smell sweet, and the corn is yellow as the summer sun, that's the garden of Clem—Farmer Clem. All day long Farmer Clem worked in the garden, hoeing, raking, and weeding.

Farmer Clem was so busy gardening that he didn't see
the tiny family that lived at the edge of the garden:
Father Mouse, Mother Mouse, and Baby Mouse.

Clem's garden was their garden too, though Farmer Clem didn't know it.

One day, while Mother and Father Mouse were busy with
the preparations for their midsummer party, Baby Mouse
wandered away.

Baby Mouse walked past the beets, corn, onions, and parsley. She came to the lettuce. Baby Mouse was tired. She was ready for her nap.

Baby Mouse climbed into a head of lettuce.

Mother called out, "BABY, WHERE ARE YOU?" Baby
didn't answer. Father yelled, "BABY, COME HOME!"
Baby didn't answer. Baby was fast asleep.

Meanwhile, Farmer Clem came out of his house to
gather vegetables for his dinner. He picked tomatoes,
he picked carrots, he picked a big zucchini, *AND*

he picked the head of lettuce
in which Baby Mouse lay fast asleep.

Mother and Father Mouse soon discovered the disaster.
They looked through Farmer Clem's kitchen window.

He was making a salad.
A SALAD?!!!
Father Mouse ran to the top kitchen shelf and peered over the big zucchini. Mother Mouse stayed behind the tomato. Clem put the head of lettuce on the cutting board. He took out his knife. He raised his knife.

Father Mouse yelled, "TIMBERRRRR!" as he pushed the big zucchini off the shelf. *THWACK!!!* It landed on Farmer Clem's head.

Father Mouse fell down the back of Clem's shirt. "JAKERS CRAKERS!!" cried Clem.

Mother reached deep into the lettuce. There was Baby, still asleep. Father Mouse fell out of Clem's shirt. He ran past the dishwasher. He ran past the blender. Father Mouse, Mother Mouse, and Baby Mouse jumped out the window,

into Clem's compost heap. *SQUISH!!!*
"JAKERS CRAKERS!!" said Father Mouse.
He pulled Mother Mouse and Baby Mouse out of the potato
peelings and stale bread, and the Mouse family ran home
as fast as they could.

The Big Tomato

After such a big adventure, Mother decided that Baby should have a bath. She filled the bathtub up with warm, soapy water and put Baby in. Then she went off to finish her last-minute preparations for the party.

Baby looked around the bathtub. There was nothing to play with. Baby wanted a ball. Baby climbed out of the bathtub and walked out the back door, back into Clem's garden.

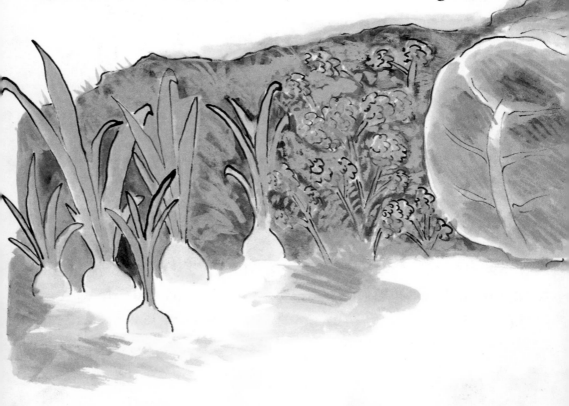

Baby walked past the beets, corn, onions, parsley, and
lettuce. Baby came to the tomatoes. She looked up at them.
They looked like balls hanging from a tree.

Baby climbed up a tomato plant and kicked one off. *SPLAT!!!* Baby thought that was fun.

Baby forgot about her bath. Baby sat in the tomato plant, kicking off tomatoes.

The guests were starting to arrive for the party. They were
all dressed up. Grandfather and Grandmother Mouse were
making their way through the vegetable garden. They walked
under the tomato plant.

SPLAT!!!! A tomato was stuck on Grandfather's head.
"MMMMMPPPPHHHHH!!!" Grandfather hopped around
the garden.

Father and Mother came out. "BABY!!!" they cried, when
they saw Baby in the tomato plant and Grandfather with his
head in a tomato. Now it was Grandfather who needed a bath.

A Mess of Peas

Soon all the guests had arrived. Everyone was in a jolly mood. They were sitting on the front porch shucking peas and looking at Baby. "What a cute baby," they all said. Mother was finishing dinner. Last of all she cooked the peas.

Then everyone gathered around the table and sat down to dinner. Baby sat in her high chair, eating peas with her fingers and drinking milk through a straw.

After dinner Baby went upstairs and fed her teddy bear peas
and milk through a straw. Then Mother tucked Baby in bed
and kissed her good night.

Baby couldn't get to sleep. Baby looked out the window.
The moon was full. Everyone was out in the garden, talking.

Baby took out her straw and started to shoot leftover peas
with it. "OUCH!!" said Grandfather. "OUCH!!" said
Grandmother. "Darn mosquitoes!!!" said Father. No one
saw Baby shooting peas in the dark.

Then Baby saw something no one else saw. Something creeping through the lettuce on tiptoe. Something with red fur and sharp teeth, hungry for little morsels of mouse. *PTTTOOOOOOIIIIII!!!* Baby shot a pea.

YEEEEEOOOOOWWWWW!!! It jumped. A FOX! Everyone ran inside. They leaned out the window and yelled at the fox. They yelled so loudly they woke up Farmer Clem. Farmer Clem ran out to the vegetable garden.

But all he saw was the fox's bushy red tail disappearing across the meadow. Farmer Clem went back to bed. Soon he was snoring as loudly as before.

Everyone went back outside. Grandfather brought out his
fiddle and tuned it up. Mother brought costumes out of the
family trunk.

Soon everyone was dressed up as vegetables. They made a circle in the middle of the garden and Grandfather started to play "The Pea Patch Jig." Everyone danced beneath the midsummer moon.

Baby wanted to be a vegetable too—a bright green pea. And she wanted to dance where the pole beans climb, where the tomatoes grow fat, where the onions smell sweet, and the corn is yellow as the summer sun.

Readers interested in hearing Dan Emmet's wonderful old tune "The Pea Patch Jig"
are recommended to the record *Vassar Clements, John Hartford, Dave Holland*
(Rounder Records, Cambridge, Massachusetts).

Very special thanks to John Hartford for his discovery, arrangement,
and musical autography of "The Pea Patch Jig."
Copyright © 1986 by John Hartford Music, B.M.I.
Reprinted by permission.

Copyright © 1986 by Thacher Hurd
All rights reserved.

Published by Crown Publishers, Inc.
225 Park Avenue South, New York, New York 10003
and represented in Canada by the Canadian MANDA Group.
CROWN is a trademark of Crown Publishers, Inc.
Manufactured in Italy

Library of Congress Cataloging-in-Publication Data
Hurd, Thacher.   The pea patch jig.

Summary: Despite being picked with the lettuce and
almost ending up in a salad, Baby Mouse refuses to stay
out of Farmer Clem's garden.
[1. Mice—Fiction   2. Gardens—Fiction]   I. Title.
PZ7.H9562Pe   1986   [E]   86-2693
ISBN 0-517-56307-X

Designed by Constance Fogler
10 9 8 7 6 5 4 3 2 1
First Edition

 A Children's Choice® Book Club Edition from Macmillan Book Clubs, Inc.

Macmillan Book Clubs, Inc. offers a wide variety of products for
children. For details on ordering, please write Macmillan Book
Clubs, Inc., 6 Commercial Street, Hicksville, N.Y. 11801.